CARTWHEELS

# Fetch the Slipper

## Sheila Lavelle

Illustrated by

**Paula Martyr**

Hamish Hamilton
London

# HAMISH HAMILTON CHILDREN'S BOOKS

Published by the Penguin Group
27 Wrights Lane, London W8 5TZ, England
Viking Penguin Inc., 40 West 23rd Street, New York, New York 10010, U.S.A.
Penguin Books Australia Ltd, Ringwood, Victoria, Australia
Penguin Books Canada Limited, 2801 John Street, Markham, Ontario, Canada L3R 1B4
Penguin Books (N.Z.) Ltd, 182–190 Wairau Road, Auckland 10, New Zealand

Penguin Books Ltd, Registered Offices, Harmondsworth, Middlesex, England

First published in Great Britain 1989 by
Hamish Hamilton Children's Books

Copyright © 1989 by Sheila Lavelle
Illustrations copyright © 1989 by Paula Martyr
1 3 5 7 9 10 8 6 4 2

British Library Cataloguing-in-Publication Data:
Lavelle, Sheila
Fetch the slipper
I. Title    II. Series
832'914 [J]

ISBN 0–241–12660–6

Typeset by Kalligraphics Ltd, Horley, Surrey
Printed in Great Britain by
Cambus Litho Ltd
East Kilbride, Scotland

Grandad came downstairs one morning
looking very cross and grumpy.

He looked as grumpy as a giraffe with
a sore throat.

5

"I've lost one of my slippers," he grumbled. "One of my best red velvet slippers, that Betty sent from America. Now what am I going to do?"

"Put your wellies on instead," said Mum.

Grandad scowled.

"Ha-ha! Very funny," he said. "You're some help, I must say!"

He sat down at the kitchen table.

Jamie and Fiona giggled into their cornflakes.

Dad poured some tea into Grandad's cup.

"Don't worry, Grandad," he said. "Benbow will find it."

Grandad scowled. "Benbow?" he said. "What, him? He's the stupidest dog in the world."

"He's very good at finding things," said Mum.

She gave Grandad a plate of bacon and eggs.

Jamie and Fiona began to shout,
"Benbow! Benbow! Where are you?"

A big collie dog with muddy paws came
running in from the garden.

He was black and white and brown,
with a bushy tail that never stopped
wagging.

Benbow liked fetching things better
than anything else in the world.

"Fetch the slipper, Benbow," said
Grandad.

Benbow wagged his tail.

He ran happily out of the kitchen and
bounded up the stairs.

Benbow was back in no time with a red velvet slipper in his mouth.

"I told you so," said Mum smugly.

Grandad looked at the slipper.

"That's the left slipper, you mutt!" he said. "It's the right one that's missing!"

Fiona giggled so much she almost choked.

Grandad flung the slipper on the floor.

Jamie buttered a slice of toast.

"Try again, Benbow," he said. "Fetch the *other* slipper."

Benbow raced out again.

He was back in no time with Jamie's
old green shirt that had no buttons on.

"I haven't seen that for years!" laughed
Jamie. "Fetch the SLIPPER, Benbow."

With a joyful bark Benbow dashed
upstairs.

This time he came back with a pink plastic lavatory brush.

"I've been looking for that for weeks!" said Mum in amazement.

Everybody laughed and Benbow galloped out again.

He came back a minute later with
Dad's red woolly nightcap.
"Now where on earth did he find that?"
said Dad, scratching his head.

"FETCH THE SLIPPER, BENBOW!"
everybody shouted together, and Benbow
raced out once more.

This was the best game he had ever
played in his life.

Soon Benbow had made a huge pile of
things on the kitchen floor.

He was puffing and panting and his
tongue was hanging out of his mouth.

But he still hadn't found Grandad's
slipper.

Jamie put his arms round Benbow's
neck.

He looked straight into the dog's eyes.

"Slipper, Benbow!" he said. "Slipper!
Fetch the SLIPPER!"

Benbow looked at Jamie, his head on
one side.

Suddenly Benbow turned and raced out of the kitchen door.

He galloped down the garden path.

He leaped over the gate and bounded down the lane towards the village.

NOW he knew what everybody wanted.

"What on earth can he be up to?" said
Mum, pouring another cup of tea.

"Something stupid, I'll bet," grumbled
Grandad.

Jamie and Fiona went out into the
garden to wait for Benbow to come back.

They didn't have to wait long.

Benbow came flying over the garden gate and raced towards the house.

Something was dangling from his jaws. Something brown and slippery.

"What can it be?" said Fiona.

Benbow sat down proudly at Jamie's feet.

Jamie took the slippery brown thing out of the dog's mouth.

He laughed so much he almost fell over.

"That's not a slipper, Benbow," he said. "It's a KIPPER!"

"Yuck!" said Fiona, making a face.

Mum gave the kipper to the cat.

"I told you Benbow was a stupid dog," snorted Grandad.

He sat in his old armchair and sulked.

Benbow looked sad and hung his head.
Jamie felt sorry for him.

"Never mind, Benbow," he said. "You did your best. Let's go and play in the garden."

Jamie threw Benbow's rubber ball down the lawn and Benbow brought it back.

"Good dog!" said Jamie.

Benbow wagged his tail.

"My turn now," said Fiona.

She threw the ball.

This time it didn't roll over the grass.

It bounced through the kitchen doorway and rolled under Grandad's chair.

"What a rotten throw!" said Jamie.

"Fetch the ball, Benbow," said Fiona.
Benbow ran into the kitchen.

He lay on the floor and put his head
under Grandad's chair.
He wriggled out with something in his
mouth.

It wasn't the ball.

It was Grandad's lost slipper.

The red velvet one that Betty had sent from America.

It had been under Grandad's chair all the time.

"Grandad!" laughed Jamie. "Benbow has found your slipper!"

Everybody hugged and patted
Benbow.

Even Grandad began to smile.

"He's the cleverest dog in the world,"
he said. "Haven't I always said so?"